P

P9-DNT-887

Fergus, M.
Buddy and Earl and the great
big baby.

PRICE: $15.00 (3798/jparp)

AUG - - 2016

For my sister Angela — MF

For my daughter Edie — CS

Text copyright © 2016 by Maureen Fergus
Illustrations copyright © 2016 by Carey Sookocheff
Published in Canada and the USA in 2016 by Groundwood Books

All rights reserved. No part of this publication may be reproduced, stored in a
retrieval system or transmitted, in any form or by any means, without the prior
written consent of the publisher or a license from The Canadian Copyright
Licensing Agency (Access Copyright). For an Access Copyright license,
visit www.accesscopyright.ca or call toll free to 1-800-893-5777.

Groundwood Books / House of Anansi Press
groundwoodbooks.com

We acknowledge for their financial support of our publishing program the Canada
Council for the Arts, the Ontario Arts Council and the Government of Canada.

 Canada Council for the Arts   Conseil des Arts du Canada   ONTARIO ARTS COUNCIL CONSEIL DES ARTS DE L'ONTARIO an Ontario government agency un organisme du gouvernement de l'Ontario   With the participation of the Government of Canada Avec la participation du gouvernement du Canada | Canada

Library and Archives Canada Cataloguing in Publication
Fergus, Maureen, author
Buddy and Earl and the great big baby / Maureen Fergus ; pictures by Carey
Sookocheff.
(Buddy and Earl ; 3)
Issued in print and electronic formats.
ISBN 978-1-55498-716-0 (bound).—ISBN 978-1-55498-717-7 (pdf)
I. Sookocheff, Carey, illustrator II. Title.
PS8611.E735B842 2016   jC813'.6   C2015-908412-1
C2015-908413-X

The illustrations were done in Acryl Gouache on watercolor paper
and assembled in Photoshop.
Design by Michael Solomon
Printed and bound in Malaysia

FSC
www.fsc.org
MIX
Paper from
responsible sources
FSC® C012700

BUDDY
and
EARL

and the great  big baby

MAUREEN FERGUS

Pictures by
CAREY SOOKOCHEFF

GROUNDWOOD BOOKS
HOUSE OF ANANSI PRESS
TORONTO   BERKELEY

ST. THOMAS PUBLIC LIBRARY

"Mrs. Cunningham is coming for a visit,"
said Mom. "She's bringing her baby with her."

"Ooh, I can't wait!" cried Meredith, who loved babies.

"Me, neither!" cried Buddy, who loved Meredith.

"Hurrah!" shouted Earl, who loved excitement of any kind.

After Earl finished cheering, he turned to
Buddy and said, "So! What's a baby?"
Buddy was very surprised by the question.

"Is a baby something you drive around in?"
asked Earl.
"No," said Buddy confidently.

"Is a baby something you plug into the wall?"
asked Earl.

"No," said Buddy, a little less confidently.

"Is a baby something delicious to eat?" asked
Earl, licking his lips.

"NO!" exclaimed Buddy in alarm.

"Babies are small and adorable," explained Buddy.

"I am small and adorable," said Earl.

"Babies like to eat things off the floor," said Buddy.

"I like to eat things off the floor," said Earl.

"Sometimes, babies smell very interesting," said Buddy.

"Sometimes, I smell very interesting!" marveled Earl. "Oh, Buddy, who would have thought that babies and hedgehogs had so much in common?"

"Not me," admitted Buddy.

Just then, the doorbell rang.

Worried that Mom hadn't heard it, Buddy ran to the door and barked and barked and barked and barked and barked.

Earl waddled after him, keen to meet this creature he'd heard so many good things about.

As soon as Mom opened the door,
Earl politely said, "Hello, baby."
The baby paid no attention to Earl.
The baby paid no attention to *anyone*.

Instead, he toddled into the living room, knocked over a vase of flowers, tore up a magazine and ripped a leg off Meredith's favorite dolly. After that, he headed for the kitchen. Filled with foreboding, Buddy and Earl chased after him.

"Babies are not small and adorable," spluttered Earl. "They are large and horrible!"

Before Buddy could disagree, the baby grabbed his favorite chew toy and started sucking on it.

"No, baby," said Buddy patiently. "You'll get your germs all over my toy."

Next, the baby reached into Earl's cage.
"NO, BABY!" roared Earl. "BAD BABY!"
Laughing, the baby grabbed a handful of
Earl's food and shoved it into his mouth.
    Earl was horrified.

When Mrs. Cunningham saw her baby
eating hedgehog food, she was also horrified.
"It's time for your nap," she told the baby.
Meredith felt very sorry for the baby.
Buddy felt a little bit sorry for the baby.
Earl didn't feel at all sorry for the baby.

"I'm glad she put you into your cage," Earl told the baby.

"That is not a cage, Earl. That is a playpen," said Buddy.

"You have no one but yourself to blame," Earl informed the baby.

The baby hollered and screamed until Meredith read him a bedtime story.

After that, he calmed down but he didn't fall asleep.

Neither did Earl.

"I'm watching you, baby," warned Earl.
The baby gave Earl a great, gummy smile.
"Awww," said Earl.
The baby blew Earl a noisy kiss.
"Tee, hee!" giggled Earl.

The baby swung one chubby leg over the side
of the playpen.
"What are you doing?" asked Earl anxiously.

Earl woke Buddy up by giving him a teensy-
weensy chomp on the tail.

"Shush or you'll wake up Meredith!"
whispered Earl. "I need your help, Buddy. The
adorable little baby has escaped!"

"I thought you said babies were large and
horrible," whispered Buddy.

Earl didn't answer. He was already
speed-waddling away.

When Earl saw that the hallway was empty, he cried, "Oh, Buddy, this is terrible. The baby could be in Meredith's room trying to swim across a swamp full of poisonous snakes!"

"I do not remember seeing a swamp full of poisonous snakes in Meredith's room!" cried Buddy.

The baby was not in Meredith's room.

"The baby could be in Michael's room trying to leap over a giant pit of bubbling lava!" bellowed Earl.

"I do not think there is a giant pit of bubbling lava in Michael's room!" bellowed Buddy.

The baby was not in Michael's room.

"There is only one possibility left!" shrieked Earl. "The baby must be in Mom and Dad's room trying to outrun a stampeding herd of dinosaurs!"

When Buddy and Earl burst into Mom and Dad's room, they did not see the baby or a stampeding herd of dinosaurs. They did, however, hear a splashing noise coming from Mom and Dad's bathroom.

Dashing over, they found the baby washing one of Dad's new shoes.

"Thank goodness," sighed Earl. "The baby is safe and all is well."

"I do not know if Dad would think that all is well, Earl," said Buddy.

"People are more important than things," said Earl wisely. "Now, go find something else for the baby to wash. We need to keep him busy until help arrives."

By the time help arrived, Dad's watch, slippers
and book were just as clean as his shoe.

"Do you know what I just realized, Buddy?" said Earl. "Babies and dogs have something in common, too."

"What is that, Earl?" asked Buddy.

"They both make the world a happier place," said Earl.

"Oh, Earl, do you really think so?" asked Buddy.

"Yes, Buddy," said Earl. "I really do."